MAR 2 4 2022
NO LONGER PROPERTY OF
SEATTLE PUBLIC LIBRARY
D0624014

by Anna Kang *illustrated by* Christopher Weyant

This Is (Not) Enough

Text copyright © 2022 by Anna Kang • Illustrations copyright © 2022 by Christopher Weyant • All rights reserved. No part of this book may be reproduced, or stored in a retrieval system, or transmitted in any form or by any means, electronic, mechanical, photocopying, recording, or otherwise, without express written permission of the publisher. • Published by Two Lions, New York • www.apub.com • Amazon, the Amazon logo, and Two Lions are trademarks of Amazon.com, Inc., or its affiliates. • ISBN-13: 9781542018517 • ISBN-10: 154201851X • The illustrations are rendered in ink and watercolor with brush pens on Arches paper. • Book design by Abby Dening • Printed in China • First Edition • 10 9 8 7 6 5 4 3 2 1

To our brave and selfless healthcare workers, first responders, essential workers, scientists, and beloved teachers. Thank you for your sacrifice, the gift of everything.

This is
not enough.

Did you find a present yet?
Not yet.

This is for my best friend!
It has to be COOL and FUN
and BIG and "WOW"!

Like *this*!

Wow!

What are you going to get?
I am not sure yet.

But it has to be
one of a kind.

And warm
and soft.

And from
the heart.

It has to be
something that
shows how
I *feel*!

I know! I am going to knit a one-of-a-kind, warm, soft, from-the-heart scarf!

Good idea!
Can you knit?
How hard
can it be?

I can't WAIT for you to see your gift!

Well, I have the BEST idea for *your* gift!

What is it?
You will find out soon enough!

This is not enough.

LATER
And then you write,
"Thank you for being my best friend!"
Roger that.

AHHHHHHH!
Never mind! EJECT!
I've *got* it!

What is all this?

You will find out
soon enough!

HOW
TO
KNIT

Sigh. This is
not good enough.

LATER

INSTANT MAGICAL GARDEN
INSTANT MAGICAL GARDEN

INSTANT MAGICAL GARDEN

EASY CAKE

BUMP!

THIS IS NOT

ENOUGH!!!

Close your eyes!

Okay, open them!

TA-DA!

You *made* this?
For *me*?
Yes!

It is so cool and fun
and big and "wow"!
I *LOVE* it!

I wanted to give you something
one of a kind. And warm.
And soft. And from the heart.

It is not enough, but all
I have is this. . . .

You *made* this?

Yes.

It is more than enough.

It is everything.

Surprise!
What did you get *us*?